Green Light Readers

For the new reader who's ready to GO!

DISCARD

Amazing adventures await every young child who is eager to read.
   Green Light Readers encourage children to explore, to imagine, and to grow
through books. Created for beginning readers at two levels of skill, these lively illustrated
stories have been carefully developed to reinforce reading basics taught at school and
to make reading a fun and rewarding experience for children and grown-ups to share
outside the classroom.
   The grades and ages within each skill level are general guidelines only, and books
included in both levels may feature any or all of the bulleted characteristics. When
choosing a book for a new reader, remember that every child progresses at his or her
own pace—be patient and supportive as the magic of reading takes hold.

1 Buckle up!
Kindergarten–Grade 1: Developing reading skills, ages 5–7
• Short, simple stories • Fully illustrated • Familiar objects and situations
• Playful rhythms • Spoken language patterns of children
• Rhymes and repeated phrases • Strong link between text and art

❷ Start the engine!
Grades 1–2: Reading with help, ages 6–8
• Longer stories, including nonfiction • Short chapters
• Generously illustrated • Less-familiar situations
• More fully developed characters • Creative language, including dialogue
• More subtle link between text and art

*Green Light Readers incorporate characteristics detailed in the Reading Recovery model
used by educators to assess the readability of texts through the end of first grade.
Guidelines for reading levels for these readers have been developed with assistance from
Mary Lou Meerson. An educational consultant, Ms. Meerson has been a classroom teacher,
a language arts coordinator, an elementary school principal, and a university professor.*

Published in collaboration with Harcourt School Publishers

The Enormous Turnip

Alexei Tolstoy

Illustrated by Scott Goto

Green Light Readers
Harcourt, Inc.
San Diego   New York   London

www.HarcourtBooks.com

First Green Light Readers edition 2002
Green Light Readers is a trademark of Harcourt, Inc.,
registered in the United States of America and/or other jurisdictions.

Library of Congress Cataloging-in-Publication Data
Tolstoy, Aleksey Konstantinovich, graf, 1817–1875.
The enormous turnip/Alexei Tolstoy; illustrated by Scott Goto.
p.   cm.
Summary: A cumulative tale in which the turnip planted by an old man grows
so enormous that everyone must help to pull it up.
[1. Turnips—Fiction.   2. Cooperativeness—Fiction.]   I. Goto, Scott, ill.   II. Title.
PZ7.T58En 2002
[E]—dc21   2001007733
ISBN 0-15-204585-6
ISBN 0-15-204584-8 pb

A C E G H F D B
A C E G H F D B (pb)

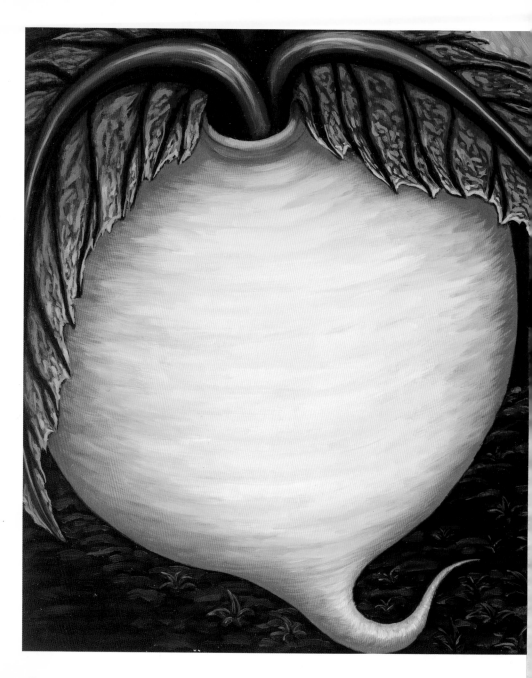

Once upon a time, an old man planted a little turnip. "Grow, grow, little turnip—grow sweet!" he said.

"Grow, grow, little turnip—grow strong!"
And the turnip grew up sweet and strong
and . . . *enormous.*

Then, one day, the old man tried to pull the turnip up. He pulled and pulled again, but he could not pull it up.

So, the old man called the old woman.

The old woman pulled the old man, the old man pulled the turnip. They pulled and pulled again, but they could not pull it up.

So, the old woman called her granddaughter.

The granddaughter pulled the old woman,
the old woman pulled the old man, the
old man pulled the turnip.

They pulled and pulled again, but they
could not pull it up.
So, the granddaughter called the black dog.

The black dog pulled the granddaughter, the granddaughter pulled the old woman, the old woman pulled the old man, the old man pulled the turnip. They pulled and pulled again, but they could not pull it up.

So, the black dog called the cat.

The cat pulled the black dog, the black dog pulled the granddaughter, the granddaughter pulled the old woman, the old woman pulled the old man, the old man pulled the turnip. They pulled and pulled again, but *still* they could not pull it up....

So, the cat called the mouse.

The mouse pulled the cat, the cat pulled
the black dog, the black dog pulled the
granddaughter, the granddaughter pulled

the old woman, the old woman pulled the
old man, the old man pulled the turnip....

And up came the enormous turnip at last!

Meet the Illustrator and Author

Scott Goto has been drawing since he was a child. His love of art makes him work very hard to be the best artist he can be. He also loves learning about history and figures from history such as Tolstoy.

Alexei Tolstoy was a writer in Russia many years ago. He wrote children's tales as well as poems, plays, and stories for grown-ups. He also wrote science fiction stories. One of them is about people who visit the planet Mars.

Look for these other Green Light Readers
in affordably priced paperbacks and hardcovers!

Level 2/Grades 1–2

Animals on the Go
Jessica Brett
Illustrated by Richard Cowdrey

A Bed Full of Cats
Holly Keller

Boots for Beth
Alex Moran
Illustrated by Lisa Campbell Ernst

Catch Me If You Can!
Bernard Most

The Chick That Wouldn't Hatch
Claire Daniel
Illustrated by Lisa Campbell Ernst

Daniel's Mystery Egg
Alma Flor Ada
Illustrated by G. Brian Karas

Digger Pig and the Turnip
Caron Lee Cohen
Illustrated by Christopher Denise

Farmers Market
Carmen Parks
Illustrated by Edward Martinez

The Fox and the Stork
Gerald McDermott

Get That Pest!
Erin Douglas
Illustrated by Wong Herbert Yee

I Wonder
Tana Hoban

Marco's Run
Wesley Cartier
Illustrated by Reynold Ruffins

The Purple Snerd
Rozanne Lanczak Williams
Illustrated by Mary GrandPré

Shoe Town
Janet Stevens and Susan Stevens Crummel
Illustrated by Janet Stevens

Splash!
Ariane Dewey and Jose Aruego

Tumbleweed Stew
Susan Stevens Crummel
Illustrated by Janet Stevens

The Very Boastful Kangaroo
Bernard Most

Where Do Frogs Come From?
Alex Vern

Why the Frog Has Big Eyes
Betsy Franco
Illustrated by Joung Un Kim

And for younger readers, look for
Level 1/Kindergarten–Grade 1 Green Light Readers

Green Light Readers
For the new reader who's ready to GO!